Devdutt Pattanaik loves to write, illustrate and lecture on the relevance of mythology in modern times. He has since 1996, written over 50 books and 1000 columns for adults and children. To know more, visit www.devdutt.com.

Sasi Edavarad is an eminent Mural Artist and a teacher. As a young child he was attracted by the intricate paintings of the temple walls. He began his study of Kerala Mural under the tutorship of Guru Sri M.K. Sreenivasan, Institute of Mural Painting, Guruvayur. He also specializes in the utilization of natural colours procured from natural elements for use in Kerala Murals. He has been blessed with the honour of painting the walls of many famed temples of Kerala.

DEVDUTT PATTANAIK

VAHANA

Gods and Their Favourite Animals

✳ Read and Colour ✳

Illustrations by the Author
Colour Rendering by Sasi Edavarad

RUPA

Published by
Rupa Publications India Pvt. Ltd 2020
7/16, Ansari Road, Daryaganj
New Delhi 110002

Sales Centres:

Allahabad Bengaluru Chennai
Hyderabad Jaipur Kathmandu
Kolkata Mumbai

ISBN: 978-93-90356-06-5

First impression 2020

10 9 8 7 6 5 4 3 2 1

The moral right of the author has been asserted.

This edition is for sale in the Indian Subcontinent only.

Design and typeset Special Effects Graphics Design Co., Mumbai
Printed by Gopsons Papers Ltd., Noida

Within infinite myths lies an eternal truth
Who sees it all?
Varuna has a thousand eyes
Indra, a hundred
You and I, only two.

A long time ago, the gods could not travel much because animals had not been born then. They had no way to travel except by walking.

They became very sad, so they went to Brahma and said, 'Oh Brahma! We want to travel around the world but we are tired of walking. When we walk, we cannot walk very far. So, can you please find a way to help us travel from one place to another?'

Brahma did not know what to do, so he went up to the goddess of knowledge called Saraswati.

She said, 'The answer is simple: you must create animals, birds and fish. They can then become friends of the gods and take the gods wherever they want to go. They can be used as vehicles and will be loved.'

Brahma agreed.

Brahma created a giant turtle called Kashyapa. He told the giant turtle to produce different kinds of animals that could travel around the world. These could then become the vahanas of the gods. Kashyapa agreed and he produced different kinds of children.

He first created creatures without legs—fish who lived in water and serpents who crawled.

His second set of children had two legs—birds who could fly and apes who could walk.

His third set of children had four legs or more—hooves, claws, toes, tentacles and more.

The animals soon became unhappy. They went to Brahma and said that it was unfair that the birds ate fish and serpents, that animals with claws could feast on animals with hooves.
It was also sad that big fish were eating small fish. This always led to terrible battles. Most lived in fear for their lives. They said that this was not correct.

Brahma told them that to stay alive all animals need energy. Some animals eat plants. Some animals eat animals. Eventually all things born have to die. This is the cycle of life.

Animals learnt and understood this. They accepted that this would never change. So, the animals went to Kashyapa and asked how they could be happy. They asked him to take away their worry of being either eaten by someone or constantly looking for someone to eat.

Kashyapa said, 'Become friends with the gods; the gods are never hungry. If you befriend the gods and stay with them all the time, you will learn the secret of how never to be hungry.'

Devdutt Pattanaik

Vahana: Gods and Their Favourite Animals

All the animals went around the world, looking for gods who could be their friends. The gods were also very happy to befriend the animals. They also were seeking help, so that they could travel around the world.

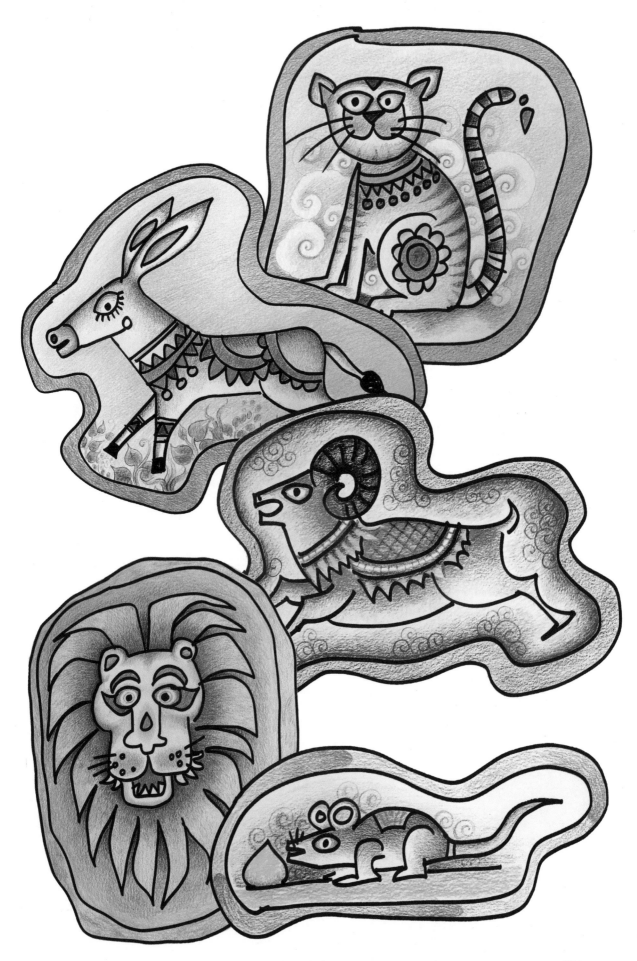

The gods needed animals to travel around the world and the animals needed the gods to learn how not to be hungry. This was an amazing idea, thanks to goddess Saraswati. This is how vahana came into being.

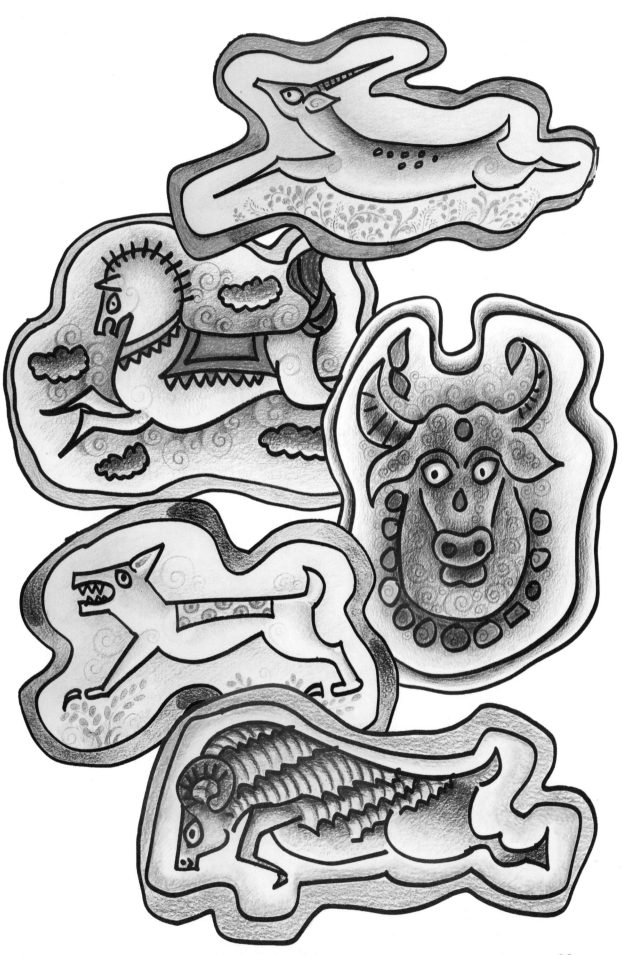

Vahana: Gods and Their Favourite Animals   19

Different animals found different gods. Let's go one by one and find out who became whose vahana.

Devdutt Pattanaik

Goose

The goose who had the ability to separate milk from water became friends with Brahma.

Separating milk from water means separating fact from fiction, truth from falsehood. As the creator, Brahma needed clarity. So the goose was a good friend to have.

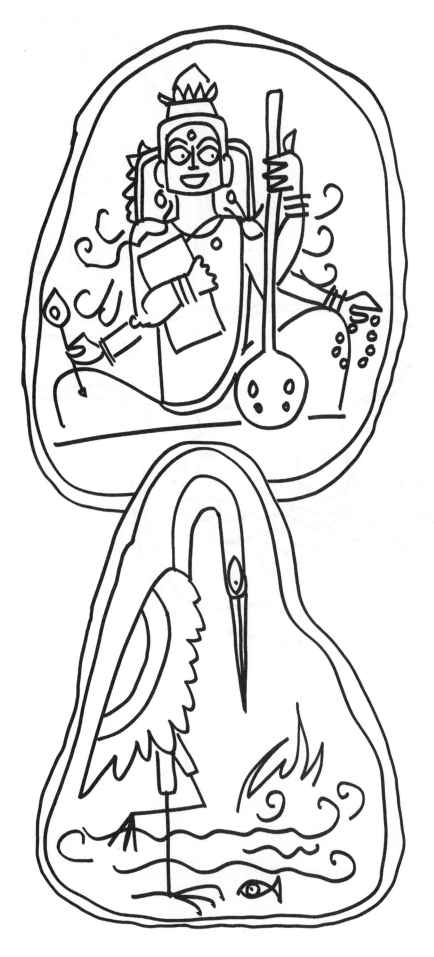

Devdutt Pattanaik

Heron

Saraswati loved knowledge, music, poetry and dance. For that, she needed concentration.

The heron became the friend of Saraswati because herons showed the signs of being able to concentrate. While it hunts fish, the heron can stand very still. Sometimes, it stands with just one foot in the water, its gaze on the surface, waiting patiently for a fish to swim by. So impressive was this concentration that Saraswati became friends with it.

Devdutt Pattanaik

Owl

Lakshmi is the goddess of wealth and fortune. People love her but no one can predict where she will go next.

The owl with its big round eyes became the friend of Lakshmi because his eyes reminded Lakshmi of gold coins.

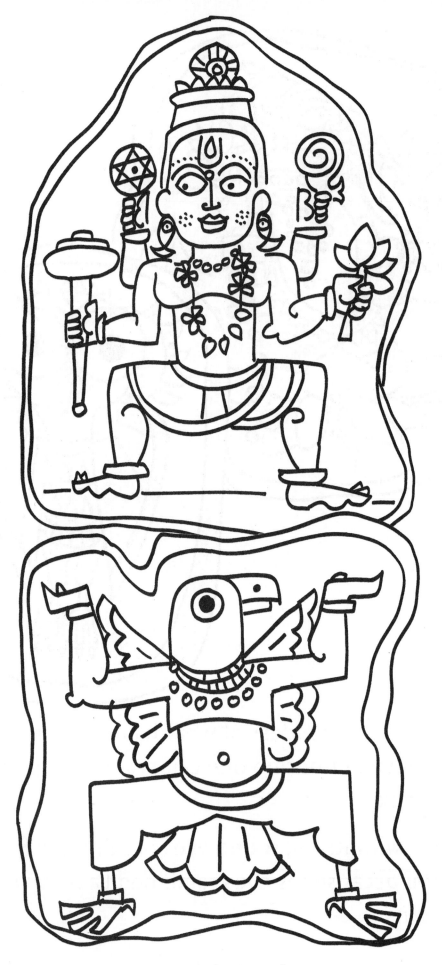

28   *Devdutt Pattanaik*

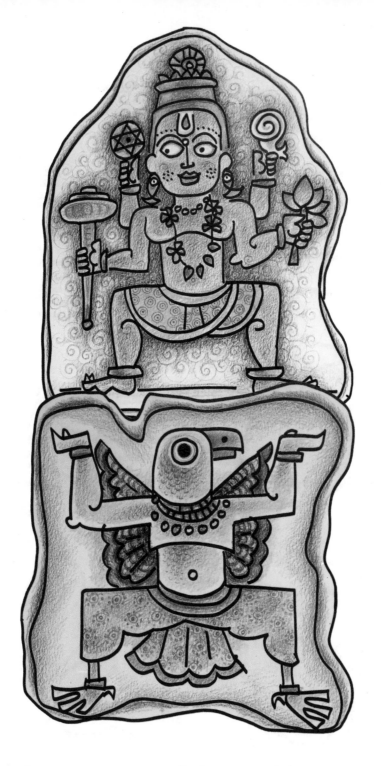

Eagle

Vishnu is the protector of the world. So he needed someone who could help him locate problems that he could solve.

Who better than an eagle—the Garuda—who can fly high in the sky and yet see the earth very clearly.

Monkey

To get rid of a troublemaker called Ravana, Vishnu took birth on earth as Ram. He had to go in exile to the forest. There, he made friends with monkeys. The smartest monkey was Hanuman.

Hanuman may look like an animal but he is greater than even many gods. Some say he is actually a form of Shiva.

Devdutt Pattanaik

Horse

When Vishnu will have to destroy a corrupt society, he will take the form of Kalki. Then he will need a fire-breathing flying horse. Together they will ride into battles.

Did you know horses were imported into India from north-west and horse traders were called Ashwa-pati?

34

Bull

The mighty bull became the friend of Shiva.

Shiva lives on a mountain covered with snow where there is nothing to eat. But it does not matter. Shiva has taught the bull the art of overcoming hunger.

The bull's name was Nandi. He was a Zebu bull, which means he had a hump.

Devdutt Pattanaik

Dog

Shiva loves the bull, but sometimes, Shiva takes the form of Bhairava, who loves dark places. When he becomes Bhairava, the dog becomes his friend.

Bhairava's dog barks and keeps watch on ghosts in dark places.

Devdutt Pattanaik

Lion

Bhairava has a companion called Kali and she loves fighting and travelling on her lion.

Kali has big red eyes, sharp teeth and a blood-thirsty look, so the lion suits her.

The wild lion that everybody is afraid of got scared on seeing Kali.

Cat

Sashti, who writes the fortune of children on their forehead, preferred the cat, because the cat takes care of kittens.

Cats love milk too just like babies.

Match the Gods with Their Vahana

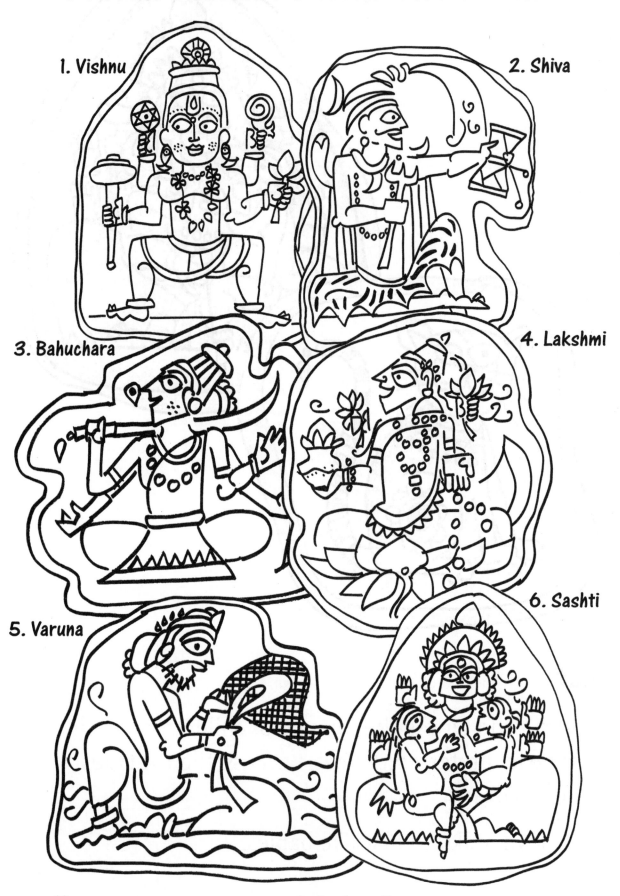

1. Vishnu

2. Shiva

3. Bahuchara

4. Lakshmi

5. Varuna

6. Sashti

Devdutt Pattanaik

a. Owl

b. Rooster

c. Bull

d. Cat

f. Eagle

e. Shark

Donkey

Shitala, the goddess who is associated with protecting children from diseases, became friends with the donkey.

The donkey works hard and watches Shitala sweep out germs and pour water to keep fever away.

Devdutt Pattanaik

Rooster

Bahuchara became friends with the rooster.

Devdutt Pattanaik

Vahana: Gods and their Favourite Animals

Rat

Ganesha chose the rat. Ganesha is the son of Shiva. He lives on Mount Kailas. No one is hungry there. So the serpent who sits around Shiva's neck never harms the rat.

The rat also does not eat the sweets on Ganesha's hand.

Devdutt Pattanaik

Peacock

Kartikeya, the other son of Shiva, is a warlord.
He travels on a peacock.

The peacock feathers have eye-like design so he can
see what others cannot see.

Devdutt Pattanaik

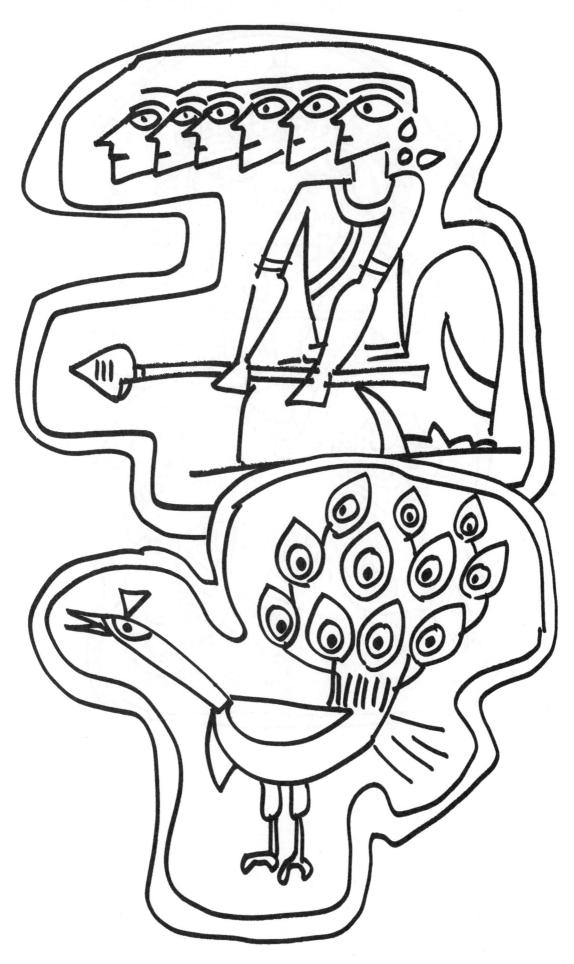

Vahana: Gods and their Favourite Animals

Tiger

A queen wanted to drink tiger milk and Ayyappa fetched it for her.

Ayyappa, the warrior-god of the south, is friends with tigers.

Devdutt Pattanaik

Shark

The great shark became the friend of Varuna, the god of the sea.

The name of this fish is Timi. She is the mother of all fishes, they say.

Devdutt Pattanaik

Dolphin

The dolphin became the friend of the bubbly Ganga who loves to dance on mountains.

Some say this is not a dolphin, but a special animal called Makara with head of an elephant and body of a fish.

Devdutt Pattanaik

Turtle

The turtle became the friend of Goddess Yamuna because Yamuna does not like to run, she likes to move slowly in life.

Devdutt Pattanaik

Elephant

The elephant became friends with Indra.

Indra is the king of gods, ruler of the sky, who releases rain by hurling thunderbolts.

The elephant has many trunks and tusks, suitable for the king of gods.

Devdutt Pattanaik

Ram

Agni, the fire god, made friends with the ram.

Agni is the messenger of the gods.

Devdutt Pattanaik

Antelope

Vayu became friends with the antelope, because an antelope runs as fast as the wind.

Devdutt Pattanaik

Parrot

The parrot became friends with Kamadev.

Kamadeva is the god of love and spring and he loves the bright green feathers of the parrot.

Devdutt Pattanaik

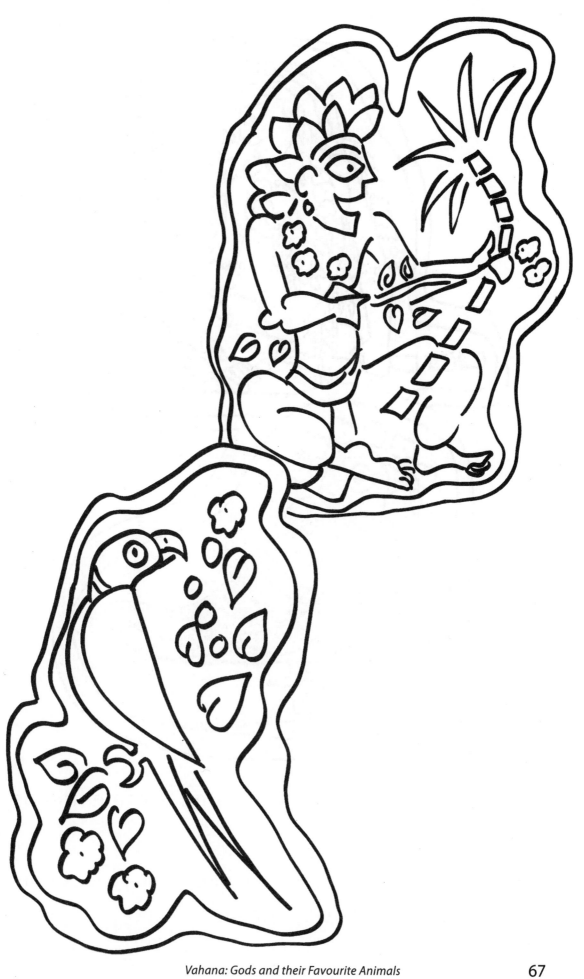

Pigeon

The pigeon who likes to fly around became friends with Ratidevi.

The pigeon noticed that Rati, like Kama, loves sweet sugarcanes and colourful flowers.

Buffalo

The slow and steady buffalo became the friend of Yama, the god of death.

Everyone is afraid of Yama. But he is the kindest god, treating the rich and the poor, the strong and the weak alike.

Devdutt Pattanaik

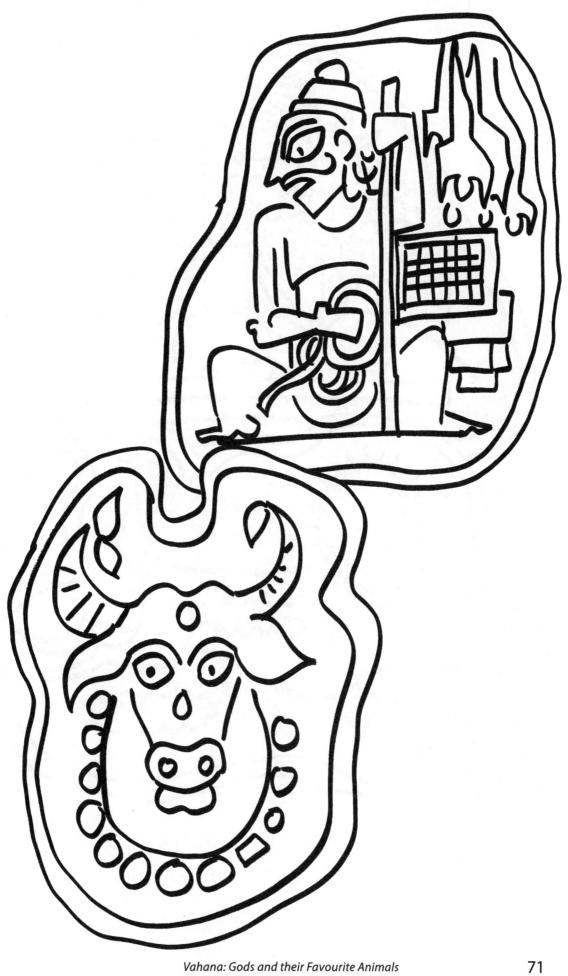

The sun in the sky said, 'I want a chariot pulled by horses'. So, seven horses came forward to pull his chariot.

Devdutt Pattanaik

Chandra, the moon god, could not make up his mind, so he had his one chariot pulled by a deer and the other chariot pulled by geese.

When you see the moon you cannot see the geese or deer as they are on the other side.

Devdutt Pattanaik

The god of the planet Mars likes to fight. He made friends with the ram, i.e. male sheep.

Male sheep keep head-butting other male sheep. That is why Mars, i.e. Mangal, likes them.

Devdutt Pattanaik

Planet Mercury or Budh is mercurial—that is, he keeps changing his form, from male to female.

His favourite animal is the yali—no one is sure if it eats vegetables or meat as it has body of a lion but head of an elephant.

Devdutt Pattanaik

Venus or Shukra is the god of creativity.

Shukra brought the horse to the Asuras, who live under the earth.

Devdutt Pattanaik

Vahana: Gods and their Favourite Animals

Jupiter or Brihaspati is the guru of devas, who live in the sky. He is the god of mathematics and logic.

Brihaspati loves to ride elephants.

Devdutt Pattanaik

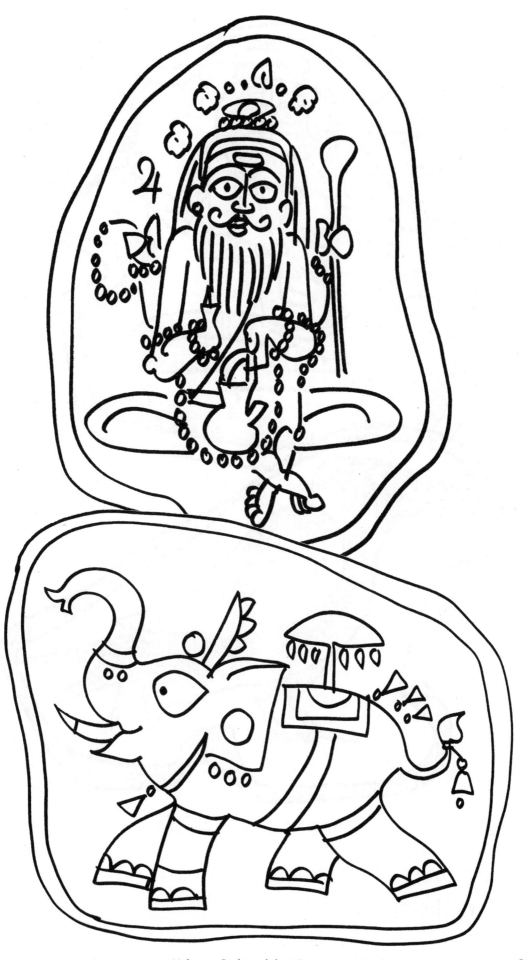

Vahana: Gods and their Favourite Animals

Saturn or Shani loves to delay things.

Saturn prefers the vulture; some say he prefers the crow.

Devdutt Pattanaik

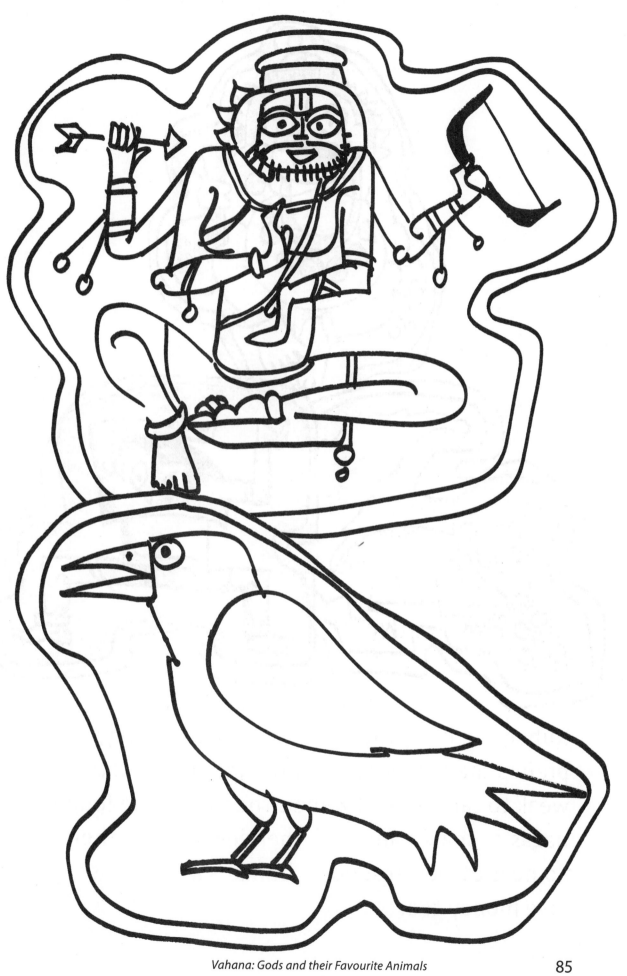

Vahana: Gods and their Favourite Animals

Kuber, the king who is obsessed with money, prefers the mongoose, but the mongoose is too weak to carry the fat Kuber. The mongoose fought nagas or snakes and took their jewels from them. So he is carried around by humans as humans love money too.

Devdutt Pattanaik

Vahana: Gods and their Favourite Animals   87

Last was Chamunda, who went to Brahma and complained, 'I don't have any pet, as all the animals have been taken!' Brahma told him, 'You will have all the pretas or ghosts as your vahana.'

So humans when alive serve Kuber but when dead and become ghosts serve Chamunda. So there is someone for everyone.

Devdutt Pattanaik

Vahana: Gods and their Favourite Animals